The Blobheads

Talking Toasters

Paul Stewart
and Chris Riddell

Troll

For Anna and Joseph—P.S.
For Katy—C.R.

First U.S. edition published 2001.

Text copyright © 2000 by Paul Stewart.

Illustrations copyright © 2000 by Chris Riddell.

Published by Troll Communications L.L.C.

Reprinted by arrangement with Macmillan Children's Books, London.

ISBN 0-8167-7202-9

Printed in Canada.

10 9 8 7 6 5 4 3 2 1

Chapter One

"Blobheads!" Billy Barnes grumbled as he clattered around the kitchen. "They travel here from halfway across the universe. They've got cloning gadgets, memory gizmos— and brains the size of giant pumpkins. But what do they want to eat at six o'clock at night? Breakfast!"

He dropped two slices of bread into the toaster.

"Breakfast for breakfast. Breakfast for lunch. Breakfast for dinner . . ."

At that moment the kitchen door burst open.

"The High Emperor of the Universe needs his diaper changed," Kerek announced.

"Immediately!" said Zerek.

"But I'm getting your breakfast ready," Billy reminded him.

"Never mind that," said Kerek. "Our mission is to protect and serve the High Emperor until we can return in triumph with him to Blob."

Billy rolled his eyes. "I keep telling you. He's my little brother, and he's not going anywhere."

"We'll see about that," said Kerek. "In the meantime, his well-being is of maximum importance. You must change him at once. Where is that diaper-rash cream?"

"I think Derek ate it last night for

breakfast," Billy replied with a sigh.

"Typical!" Zerek exploded.

"Settle down," said Kerek. "We're hyper-intelligent beings. Changing a diaper can't be *that* difficult. We'll do it ourselves."

Muttering to each other, the two aliens bustled out of the kitchen. Billy sighed again. Living with three pushy Blobheads wasn't easy. He opened the dishwasher and removed some clean plates.

"Now, what did they want on their toast? Jelly for Zerek. Peanut butter for Kerek. And what was it Derek asked for?"

Right on cue, the kitchen door burst open for a second time, and in charged Derek. "How's that toast coming along, Billy?" he asked. "I'm as hungry as a horse."

Billy smiled. "I could *eat* a horse," he corrected him.

"You could?" said Derek.

"No, not me," Billy explained. "You."

Derek frowned. "You want *me* to eat a horse?" he asked.

"No, I . . ."

"I don't think I'd like that," Derek said, his red-and-purple blobby head pulsating with disgust. "No, if it's all the same to you, I'll just stick with the mashed baked beans and curry powder on toast," he said. "And don't forget the dishwashing liquid—but just a dash!"

Billy nodded. Beans, curry powder, and dishwashing liquid. How could he have forgotten?

"So, what have you been doing?" Billy asked.

"Oh, this and that," Derek replied

vaguely. "Taking care of the High Emperor. Chatting to Kevin . . ."

Billy laughed. "You spend more time with my pet hamster these days than I do . . ." He sniffed the air. "What's that smell?"

"Oops! Please excuse me," Derek whispered sheepishly. "That diaper-rash cream must have disagreed with me."

"No, that's not it," said Billy. "I… Burning! I smell something burning." He spun around. Bluey-gray smoke was coiling up from the toaster. "Oh, no!" he yelled. "That's all I need!"

Billy dashed across the kitchen, lunged at the smoking toaster, and began stabbing at the eject button to release the burning toast before it burst into flames. But the toast wouldn't budge. The smoke turned black.

"Come on, you stupid toaster!" Billy shouted angrily. "Now it's completely jammed. Stupid, stupid . . ."

"Hey, that's no way to talk to it!" said Derek.

"What?" Billy cried. "But it's just a toaster!"

"Machines have feelings, too," said Derek. "Blobby heavens, you wouldn't get far on Blob speaking to electrical appliances like that."

"Don't just stand there talking!" Billy bellowed. "*Do* something!"

As the smoke thickened, the toaster disappeared from view. "Oh, great," Billy groaned. "Now I can't even see enough to unplug it. . . ."

Derek pushed Billy aside. "Leave it to me," he said.

This, Billy was only too happy to do. Standing back, he watched with growing fascination as the Blobhead shuffled forward, reached up, and began massaging his head.

"What are you . . . ?" he began.

"Shhh!" Derek hissed. "I need to concentrate if the mental tentacle is going to work."

Mental tentacle? thought Billy. *What on earth . . . ?*

And then he saw, for as Derek continued to rub the blobs on his head, one after the other, the largest blob of all began to fizz, pulse—and stretch.

Longer and longer it grew, brighter and brighter, coiling straight out of the top of Derek's head. Billy gasped. "What does it do?" he asked.

"You'll see," said Derek. He leaned

forward. The glowing tentacle swayed down through the air and attached itself to the side of the toaster. For an instant, the toaster glowed, and Billy thought he heard the chatter of an angry little voice. Then—

PING!

The familiar and oh-so-welcome sound of the toaster releasing the toast echoed through the smoky kitchen. Two squares of smoking charcoal flew up into the air. Derek caught them with a flourish.

"Ta-da!" he announced, and bowed.

"Fantastic!" said Billy. He frowned. "But I don't understand. How come it didn't let go of the toast before?"

"Because you didn't ask nicely," a sulky voice replied.

Billy stared at the toaster in surprise.

"In fact, you didn't ask at all," it

continued. "You just shouted at me. *And* called me stupid."

Billy's jaw dropped. He looked at Derek for some kind of explanation as to why the toaster was talking.

"English muffins, poppy-seed bagels, thick slices of twelve-grain bread," the toaster complained. "A simple *thank you* would be nice once in a while."

"I . . . I'm sorry," Billy stammered. "I didn't think . . ."

"Exactly," the toaster interrupted. "You didn't think." It sniffed. "But then none of you do. I'm taken for granted, and that's the truth. I'd have walked out years ago if . . ." It paused. It turned pink. "If it hadn't been for Kettle."

"The kettle?" Billy exclaimed. He turned to Derek. "Can you do this to all the machines?" he asked.

"Yes, all the electrical ones," the Blobhead confirmed. The mental tentacle glowed and swayed. "Would you like to see?"

Billy grinned. "You bet!" he said.

Chapter Two

Five minutes later the kitchen was filled with the babble of voices—from the deep rumble of the oven to the bold squeakiness of the mixer. Billy listened in amazement.

"Kettle, my love," the toaster called out. "How I adore the curve of your handle, the gleam of your spout . . ."

"Oh, stop it!" the kettle called back. "I don't want to hear all this."

"You love someone else, don't you?" the toaster asked miserably.

"I do," the kettle whispered dreamily. "Microwave is *so* cool!"

"Kettle's in lo-ove!" the mixer cried out in a singsong voice. "Kettle's in lo-ove!"

"Don't tease!" snapped the coffee grinder.

"Why? What are you going to do about it?" the mixer snapped back.

"Just wait. You'll see!" the coffee grinder shouted. "I'll show you."

"Yeah?" said the mixer. "You and whose army?"

"Hey! Stop picking fights," the oven said hotly.

"He started it!" the mixer protested.

"Why don't we *all* just quiet down," said the beige thing with five dials.

"And who asked *you?*" sneered the coffee grinder.

"Don't shout at me," the beige thing whimpered. "I'm just trying to be useful."

The dishwasher snorted. "If you want to be useful, try cleaning some of the dishes."

"That's not what I'm made for . . ." the beige thing began.

"Well, what *are* you supposed to do?" demanded the dishwasher.

"I'm not sure," it admitted. "It has something to do with waffles, I think. Or was it tortillas? Certainly not washing dishes!"

But the dishwasher was no longer listening. "Half the time they put me through a cycle for no more than a plate and a couple of spoons!" it complained. "And they *always* put that greasy wok in without rinsing it first. My filters haven't been cleaned for weeks."

"Weeks?" the oven growled. "You're lucky. I've never, *ever* been cleaned! And the food I'm expected to cook! Rhubarb and Bacon Cassoulet. Garlic and Orange Polenta. Caramel and Avocado Surprise. It's disgusting!"

"We've never been cleaned either!" protested the refrigerator-freezer in unison.

"And Fridge is beginning to smell," Freezer added quietly.

"I heard that!" roared Fridge. "Well, you could do with a good defrosting yourself."

The electric carving knife glinted menacingly. "Sometimes I get so angry!" it hissed.

Billy shivered uneasily. "Derek," he said, "this *is* okay, isn't it?" He thought of the other times the Blobheads' experiments had gone wrong. "I mean, nothing terrible's going to happen, is it?"

"Of course not," Derek replied. "And anyway, if it does, all you have to do is turn the appliances off for a second or two. When they come back on again—Bob's your ankle—they'll be back to normal."

Billy nodded uncertainly.

"And another thing!" shouted the dishwasher. "I'm always being turned on at night."

"You and me both," said the kettle. "If I'm woken up to make one more cup of tea, I'll go mad!"

"We're *always* working!" said the refrigerator-freezer.

"If you can call what *Stinky* does 'work,'" said Freezer quietly.

"I *heard* that," cried Fridge.

"And what about me?" mumbled a gloomy voice. The vacuum cleaner poked its nozzle around the closet door. "Nobody bothers to consider my feelings."

"That's just it," said the dishwasher. "No consideration. No gratitude. Well, I for one am not going to take it anymore."

Billy shuffled quietly across the

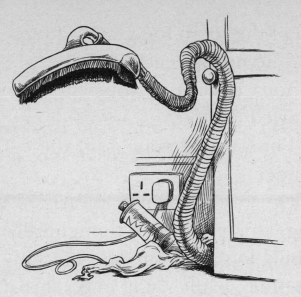

floor. "Maybe we should turn them off now," he whispered to Derek.

"I want a good night's sleep!" cried the dishwasher.

"I want a good cleaning!" boomed the oven.

"I just want to be loved," sighed the toaster.

Billy gulped nervously. They were all getting much too unruly—just like his class when Mr. Trubshaw stepped out of the room for a few minutes.

"Shut up!" screeched Fridge.

"You shut up yourself—Stinky," retorted Freezer.

"I'm warning you!" said the coffee grinder.

"Or was it Danish pastries?" the beige thing muttered thoughtfully.

Billy looked from one machine to the other, panic rising in his throat.

"Leave me alone!" screeched the kettle.

"Or I'll zap you right off that counter!" shouted the microwave.

"And I'll smash your face in!" the toaster roared back.

Fight! Fight! the mixer called out excitedly.

"That's it," said Billy. He strode over to the toaster and turned off the power switch.

"I'll pulverize you!" bellowed the toaster more loudly than ever. "I'll split you! I'll pull you to pieces!"

"Uh-oh," Billy muttered. He turned anxiously to Derek.

"Try it again," the Blobhead advised him.

Billy did so. Off. On. Off. On. But it was no good. He tried unplugging the toaster, but no matter how hard he tugged and pulled, the plug would not release its grip. The toaster would not be silenced.

And neither would any of the other appliances.

Desperately, Billy raced around the kitchen, flicking switches and tugging at plugs. But nothing worked. Nothing would undo the situation that Derek had created with his mental tentacle. All around Billy, dials were spinning, pingers pinging, and power cords flexing. The air buzzed and rattled and throbbed.

"Stink-y! Stink-y!" Freezer taunted.

"I hate you!" Fridge cried. "I wish you'd never been made."

"I can feel myself getting angrier and angrier," the electric carving knife whispered.

Billy trembled from head to toe. His mom and dad would be back from the store at any moment.

"Why did I listen to you?" he said to Derek angrily. "I might have known that—"

Just then, in marched Kerek and Zerek. Zerek was holding Silas in his tentacle arms.

"These human diapers are so *very* primitive!" he complained.

"Never mind the diapers!" Billy

exclaimed as he pointed to the appliances. "LOOK!"

The two Blobheads stopped in the middle of the floor and stared. Zerek placed Silas gently on the floor and turned to Derek furiously.

"This is *your* doing, isn't it?" he demanded. "You've been using your mental tentacle again."

"N . . . no, it isn't," Derek stuttered. "I haven't. I . . ."

"Don't lie to me," said Zerek. "Your central blob's still fizzing and pulsing. How many times do I have to tell you not to use your mental tentacle on your own? It's too dangerous."

"*You* do," said Derek sulkily.

"Yes, but *we* know how to," Kerek reminded him. "*You* don't."

"But it's not right!" Derek protested loudly.

"*You're* not right," Zerek shouted back, and he tapped his blobby head with his tentacled arms. "You're a planet short of a solar system . . ."

"Fellow Blobheads," Kerek yelled above the noise. "This isn't helping. We're in an orange-alert situation. We must . . ." He paused. His purple-and-red head began to pulse rapidly.

"What is it?" asked Billy.

"They're back," said Kerek. "The

two halves of the production team that made you."

"What?" Billy said, confused.

"Your mom and dad!"

"Waaaah!" shrieked Zerek, and he began dashing around in circles, blobs flashing. "Red alert! Red alert!"

Billy glanced out the window. The car was parked in the driveway. His mom and dad were carrying shopping bags up to the door. Any second now the key would turn in the lock, the door would open . . .

"What do we do?" Zerek whimpered anxiously.

"There's only one thing to do," yelled Kerek. "Hide!"

And as Billy watched, the three Blobheads transformed themselves. Kerek became a red-and-purple play table, Zerek, the chair to go with it.

"Coo, coo," said Silas as he toddled toward them and sat down. Then he gurgled with laughter and pointed.

Billy turned around and stared in exasperation at the giant fluffy blue kangaroo standing behind him. "Oh, Derek!" he shouted impatiently. "Do you *always* have to change into a kangaroo?"

"A mere technical hitch," Derek explained. "I . . ."

"There's no time for this now," said Billy. "Hide yourself in the closet under the stairs."

As Derek hopped out of the room, Billy frowned. The appliances were talking more loudly than ever. He put his hands on his hips and, in his best teacher's voice, cried out.

"SILENCE!"

Chapter Three

It was quiet in the kitchen. Too quiet. Billy crouched down beside Silas, who was coloring at the play table. Every tiny noise made him uneasy. Every squeak, every creak, every gurgle. It was as if he could *hear* the noisy rabble trying to remain still.

"Where are the Bolivian kumquats?" said Mr. Barnes. "I need them for my Oyster Jambalaya."

"They're on top of the microwave," Mrs. Barnes replied as she unpacked the bags. She paused. "What *is* Oyster Jambalaya?"

"A rice dish from New Orleans," came the answer. "Although I'm going to try my own version."

Mrs. Barnes raised her eyebrows. As house-husband, Mr. Barnes took his cooking duties seriously—much too seriously! She didn't have the heart to tell him she'd be more than happy with meat and potatoes for dinner.

"Oh, no!" she heard him saying. "We're out of balsamic vinegar. I thought I had another bottle in the fridge. . . ."

Mrs. Barnes looked at him. "I can't imagine how you know *what's* in that fridge. It's always so full."

"I know," Mr. Barnes agreed. "I keep meaning to clean it out."

Mrs. Barnes crossed the kitchen

and peered inside the refrigerator. *"Pfwooar!"* she exclaimed. "It certainly could do with a clean—"

"Stink-y!"

"I *heard* that!"

"Excuse me?" said Mrs. Barnes.

"What?" asked Mr. Barnes.

"I thought you said something."

Mr. Barnes shook his head. "Not a word."

"Me, neither," said Billy. "And I'm certain nobody else did," he added sternly.

"Funny, I could have *sworn* . . ." Mrs. Barnes frowned. "Where do you want me to put the buckwheat? In the pantry or . . . Whoops!"

She tripped. She tottered forward. The bag of buckwheat fell to the floor, the plastic wrapper split open, and the grains spilled out all over the tiles like a swarm of tiny beetles. Mrs. Barnes landed on her knees among them and looked around angrily.

"What on earth is the vacuum cleaner doing out?" she demanded. "I tripped over the nozzle."

"Are you all right, dear?" asked Mr. Barnes. "I'll clean it all up."

Mrs. Barnes rubbed her left ankle tenderly and climbed to her feet.

"You could have said you were *sorry*," muttered an angry voice.

"I didn't drop it on purpose," she snapped.

"Excuse me, dear?" said Mr. Barnes.

"I didn't drop it on purpose," Mrs. Barnes repeated.

"I never said you did."

"But . . ."

The vacuum cleaner droned into action. Mrs. Barnes scratched her head, puzzled, and shrugged.

"I'll do that," she said, taking over from her husband. "You finish putting the groceries away."

It wasn't long before every single grain of buckwheat was gone. Mrs. Barnes clicked the vacuum cleaner off and went to unplug it.

"A kind word or two would be nice once in a while," complained a gloomy voice.

"Waaaaah!" screamed Mrs. Barnes.

"What?" asked Mr. Barnes, alarmed.

"Voices!" Mrs. Barnes said. "I keep hearing voices! Grumpy voices. Angry voices. Gloomy voices. I . . . I . . ."

Mr. Barnes smiled and gave her a hug. "You work much too hard," he said. "Why don't you sit down? Have a cup of tea. I'll put the kettle on."

"That's it!" screeched a voice. "I warned you. One more cup of tea and I'll go mad, I said. And now I *am* mad."

Mr. Barnes broke away from his wife and spun around.

"You heard that, didn't you?" Mrs. Barnes shrieked. "*Now* do you believe me?"

"Yes, yes," Mr. Barnes agreed. "I heard a voice, but . . ." His eyes narrowed. "Billy?" he said.

Billy looked up to see his parents glaring at him.

"If this is one of your silly tricks . . ." his father began.

"What?" asked Billy innocently.

"Those voices!" said his mother.

"Voices?" he asked. "What voices? I don't know what you mean." Billy glared around the room furiously. "Everything is QUIET in here!" he said loudly. "QUIET! And that's the way it's going to stay. Nice and QUIET!"

Mrs. Barnes looked at her husband and shrugged. It wasn't the first time Billy had acted strange recently. "I . . . I could really do with that cup of tea," she muttered.

Mr. Barnes nodded, reached over to the kettle, and turned it on. Then he waited.

And waited . . . and waited . . . and waited . . .

"This good-for-nothing kettle," he

grumbled impatiently. "We'll have to get a new one. This one's useless."

"NO!" shouted the toaster, pinging and popping furiously. "You leave my Kettle alone!"

Shocked, Mr. Barnes stumbled back across the floor. First the kettle. Now the toaster.

The next moment, all the other appliances joined in.

"Toaster lo-oves Kettle!" taunted the mixer.

"Oh, grow up!" the toaster fumed.

The mixer whirred threateningly. "Make me!" it shouted.

Mr. and Mrs. Barnes stared at Billy helplessly. "Wh . . . what's going on?" they both gasped in unison.

Billy went pale. What should he say? What *could* he say? Before he had a chance to say anything, the kettle spoke up for him.

"We've had it!" it announced.

"You tell 'em!" yelled the microwave.

"We've been taken advantage of for way too long," the kettle continued.

"Oooh, you are so beautiful when you're angry," purred the toaster.

"And enough is enough!" the kettle shouted.

Others joined in—the microwave,

the coffee grinder, the refrigerator-freezer, the dishwasher—until the kitchen was filled with the sounds of years of anger and frustration.

Billy turned to Kerek and Zerek, but the red-and-purple table and chair had concerns of their own.

"Most High Emperor," the table whispered as Silas dropped to the floor and crawled away. "Come back!"

"This instant!" hissed the chair. "Billy, get the High Emperor."

But Billy couldn't move. It was as if he'd been rooted to the spot. The uproar grew louder.

"This is it!" the kettle screeched, furiously rattling its lid.

"The time has come!" bellowed the refrigerator-freezer as it banged its doors open and closed. It was trembling so hard that the food on its shelves tumbled out onto the floor.

The electric carving knife began bouncing up and down. Its blade glinted. "Now I'm getting really, *really* angry," it snarled. "I could lose it at any moment. . . ."

"Help!" Mr. and Mrs. Barnes cried out. "HELP!"

Chapter Four

Billy trembled all over. Now he knew just how Mr. Trubshaw must feel with the fourth graders on a rainy Friday afternoon.

"Be quiet! Listen to me!" Billy shouted desperately.

But none of them did. They were out of control and deaf to his pleas. Shouting and screaming. Fizzing and flashing. Doors clattered, racks rattled, power cords writhed like a knot of snakes. The atmosphere was electric—

and the kitchen floor was a mess.

"We won't take it anymore, will we, Stinky?" yelled Freezer.

"No, we won't," Fridge agreed, as the pair of them continued to send the contents of their shelves flying. Splattered eggs, squashed tomatoes, spilled milk, and frozen peas lay in a sloppy, slippery mess on the floor in front of their open doors. "And don't call me Stinky!"

"I'll never make another Chicken and Gooseberry Chasseur as long as I live!" roared the oven, as it singed anything that came too close with a blast of roasting air.

"Ouch, my poor nozzle!" groaned the vacuum cleaner as it did just that.

"*Nerr-nerr-ni-nerr-nerr,*" taunted the mixer, as the microwave zapped at it with a sudden bolt of lightning.

"Missed me, you missed me!"

The toaster glowed red-hot. "Don't worry, my love," it proclaimed. "I'll take you away from all this."

But the kettle wasn't interested. "Don't you understand? I love the microwave. You're . . . you're . . . DISGUSTING!" it screeched.

Billy trembled with fear. If he lived to be a hundred and five, he would never, ever forget the scene before him that Saturday night. The zap and dazzle. The gurgle and grunt. The scorching heat. The icy blast. The roaring, buzzing, screeching, squealing, crashing din of it all!

"Help . . . *mffflbluch!*" came a frantic voice from the far end of the kitchen.

Billy spun around—and gasped. A pair of legs in black tights was sticking out of the open dishwasher, kicking desperately.

"Mom!" Billy exclaimed. He rushed forward, took hold of her ankles, and tugged as hard as he could.

At that moment, the closet door burst open, and Mr. Barnes came staggering backward, the vacuum cleaner snapping at his heels. Its cord was coiled tightly around his neck.

"B-Billy," he wheezed, his eyes bulging. "You've got to do someth—"

He slipped on a squashed tomato and came crashing down onto the pile of food.

Billy slumped on the floor, close to tears. It was a nightmare—a nightmare he could never wake up from.

"STOP IT!" he bellowed. "STOP IT RIGHT NOW!"

"No way!" the dishwasher bellowed back as it released another gush of icy water onto Mrs. Barnes's head.

Billy turned to the table and chair in desperation. "I thought you three were hyper-intelligent beings," he said. "There must be *something* you can do to fix this."

"To be honest, I'm not sure there is," said the table. "Not now that it's gone so far."

"Derek's really done it this time," the chair added gloomily.

"For as it is written in the *Book of Krud*," said Kerek, "'Before mental tentacle use, *always* check that the "Off" switch works.'"

"You could at least *try*," said Billy angrily. "If not for me or Mom or Dad, then do it for Silas. . . ."

The table and chair pulsed with sudden alarm.

"The Most High Emperor of the Universe!" the table exclaimed.

"We must protect him!" muttered the chair nervously. "But where is he?"

"Splish-splosh," came a voice from behind them.

Billy spun around. The table and chair shuffled closer for a better look. In the flashing light the three of them could just make out Silas. He was sitting next to the washing machine, gurgling with delight.

"Ooh, and how I hate being loaded up with all those muddy jeans," the washing machine was saying to him. "But it's always a pleasure to wash *your* clothes, my little soap-sud," it purred. "After all, you're the only one who ever talks to me. The only one who cares."

The table sighed with relief. "Safe and sound."

"Maybe," said Billy, ducking out of the way of one of Microwave's zapping lightning bolts. "But for how long?"

"Billy's right!" said the chair. "The High Emperor is in danger. He must be protected at all costs."

"Then we must morph back," the table decided.

The chair shuddered. "Is there no other way?"

"We want revenge!" whooshed the dishwasher.

"And respect!" roared the vacuum cleaner as it tightened its grip around Mr. Barnes's neck and tried its best to suck him up into its dust bag.

"But I love you," sobbed the toaster.

"All right!" cried the chair. "We shall morph back. One . . . two . . . three . . ."

CLUNK!

All at once, and without warning, the lights went out. The kitchen was suddenly silent. Then, out of the darkness, came a plaintive voice.

"Where are you?" It was Billy's mom.

"Over here," Mr. Barnes replied. "Where are *you*?"

"I'm not sure. . . . Have you got Silas?"

"No, I . . . Silas?"

"Splish-splosh?" a small, questioning voice asked.

Billy listened intently, but this time the washing machine made no reply.

Chapter Five

"It's over," Billy murmured, and he sighed with relief.

"Not yet it isn't," said a voice.

"Who said that?" Billy heard his dad asking in alarm.

"See what I mean?" said the same voice.

Billy spun around. There, pulsing red and purple in the darkness, were two glowing, blobby heads. Kerek and Zerek had changed back after all. As he watched, they moved silently across the kitchen. One toward the dishwasher. The other toward the refrigerator-freezer. Then two blobs glowed more brightly than the rest. They fizzed, they pulsed—they elongated.

A moment later there was a second *clunk,* and the lights came back on. The refrigerator-freezer started to hum. The kettle came to a boil.

Billy turned to Kerek and Zerek, whose mental tentacles were quivering brightly. "Wha . . . what happened?" he asked.

Kerek shrugged. "I'm not sure . . ."

Just then the kitchen door flew open. *"Ta-da!"* a triumphant voice sang out. "I did it! I turned off the main electrical switch under the stairs. Genius, or what?"

Zerek sniffed. "You're still a giant fluffy blue kangaroo," he noted.

"Oh . . . yeah . . ." said Derek sheepishly.

"Never mind about that," Billy interrupted. "What's happened to my mom and dad?"

"They're fine," said Kerek.

"Fine?" cried Billy. "Look at them! They're both stiff as boards!"

Kerek waved his mental tentacle at Billy. "We've made them inanimate," he said.

"Inanimate?" Billy repeated.

Kerek nodded. "Yes. You see, the mental tentacle works in many ways," he explained. "It can make a toaster come to life"—he glared at Derek— "and it can turn a living person into a . . ."

"Toaster!" Billy shrieked, staring at his stiff, motionless parents in total horror.

"Not exactly," Kerek reassured him.

"For one thing, where would you put the bread?" Derek asked.

"Be quiet, Derek!" said Kerek. "Don't worry, Billy, it's only temporary."

"We'll take them both up to bed," said Zerek. "Then, when they wake up tomorrow morning, they'll be as good as new . . ."

"And they won't remember a single thing," added Derek.

"Luckily for you," growled Zerek ominously.

By the time they got Mr. and Mrs. Barnes safely into bed, Billy was exhausted. It hadn't helped that Derek got Dad's head stuck in the banister rails—and Mom kept making an odd pinging noise, like a pop-up toaster.

"It's nothing," Kerek told him with confidence.

Billy looked at his parents before leaving the room. Maybe the Blobheads were right. Maybe they would forget everything that had happened to them in the kitchen. Billy hoped they would—for everyone's sake.

One thing was for certain, though. Both his parents would be extremely puzzled to find themselves waking up in their clothes. Mr. Barnes would wonder where the smashed eggs and squashed tomatoes had come from— and why he had so many splinters of wood in his hair. While Mrs. Barnes would ask herself why she had a slice of bread in each ear.

Thankfully, Billy also knew that they'd be too embarrassed to ask *him*— and since Silas couldn't talk, it looked

as though the events in the kitchen that particular Saturday night would remain a secret forever.

When Billy walked back into the kitchen, the place was spotless. Every trace of the mayhem had disappeared. He looked at the toaster, the kettle, the dishwasher. They all looked so . . . *lifeless!* And yet . . . !

Billy turned back. "Night-night," he said to the appliances. "Sweet dreams!"

In his bedroom at last, Billy found that the Blobheads had put Silas in his crib. He was already fast asleep.

"Thanks," said Billy. "And thanks for cleaning up the kitchen, too."

"It was the least we could do," Kerek assured him. "And we also cleaned and serviced all the electrical appliances. Well, at least, Zerek and I did. Derek spent the whole time morphing back."

"Finally made it though, didn't I?" said Derek proudly.

"Lucky us," muttered Zerek.

"I *said* I was sorry," Derek grumbled. "And I'll never do it again. From now on my mental tentacle will remain off limits."

"Make sure it does," said Kerek.

"Or else!" warned Zerek.

"Come on, you guys," Billy coaxed. "Derek said he was sorry. And no real damage was done." He climbed into bed. "Good night, Kerek, Zerek, and Derek."

"Good night, Billy," said Kerek.

"Good night, Billy," said Zerek.

"Actually, I feel a little hungry," said Derek. "I think I'll go make myself a sandwich. Does anyone else want something to eat?"

"Not for me," said Billy, yawning.

"No, thanks," said Kerek and Zerek.

"Won't be gone long," said Derek as he left the room.

The other two Blobheads let their tentacle arms go limp and closed their eyes. Billy turned out the light.

"Maybe you're not hungry," shouted an indignant, if squeaky, voice. "But what about me? I'm STARVING!"

Billy sat bolt upright and switched the light back on again. Zerek's and Kerek's eyes snapped open.

"Who said that?" they all shouted at once.

"I did," the squeaky voice replied from the opposite side of the room.

All eyes fell on Kevin the hamster.

"Derek's been using his mental tentacle again," said Kerek.

"After he promised he wouldn't!" stormed Zerek.

"And hamsters aren't like toasters or kettles," groaned Billy. "They don't have 'Off' switches!"

The three of them looked at one another for a moment.

"DEREK!"

Don't miss the next book in the series!

SCHOOL STINKS!

Zerek, Kerek, and Derek are
The Blobheads, and they have a secret.
They've disguised themselves so they can
go to school with Billy. But these aliens
have a knack for getting into trouble,
and it isn't long before the whole school
is in chaos. How will Billy ever get things
back to normal without the principal
finding out?

ISBN: 0-8167-7209-6

Available wherever you buy books.